ID0982670

The New Series Canada

"Street SCENE"

a novel

by

PAUL KROPP

H·I·P Books

National Library of Canada Cataloguing in Publication Data

Kropp, Paul 1948–
[Riot on the street]
    Street scene / Paul Kropp.

(New Series Canada)
Previously published under title: Riot on the street.
ISBN 0-9731237-1-0

I. Title. II. Title: Riot on the street. III. Series.

PS 8571.R772R56 2002   jC813'.54   C2002-903561-9
PZ7

General editor: Paul Kropp
Text Design: Laura Brady
Illustrations redrawn by: Matt Melanson
Cover design: Robert Corrigan

    2 3 4 5 6 7   07 06 05 04 03

Printed and bound in Canada

High Interest Publishing is an imprint of the Chestnut Publishing Group

The guys weren't looking for trouble. Maybe Dwayne did pick the wrong girl to dance with. But did that give Sal and his gang an excuse to come after them? The fight should never have started – and it should never have ended the way it did.

CHAPTER 1

Eyes at the Dance

Dwayne always wanted to be somebody. The rest of us, Sammy and Jo-Jo and me, we always knew we weren't going to amount to much. But not Dwayne. He had these big dreams. He kept saying that someday he was going to buy a Maserati, or play for the Blue Jays, or get a big house someplace. Dwayne used to talk about all that stuff, and now . . . now he's never going to see any of it.

Of course, it all started from nothing. Just a Saturday afternoon downtown. We were all going to the CITY-TV dance show for some fun. We had done the audition on Thursday, and all of the guys made the cut. So now we were dressed to look real cool for the cameras – and for the girls, too.

I had on this shirt my dad sent me for my sixteenth birthday, and these Gap jeans I got real cheap from my cousin. I looked pretty good, for a tall, skinny guy with too-big feet.

Jo-Jo was wearing lots of black, but he had these chains and things to make him look like a serious dude. Sammy was so small that nothing really looked good on him. He looked like a kid who was always wearing hand-me-downs from some older brother. But Sammy was still trying. He had on his best pair of Converse runners and a shirt that felt like real silk.

But Dwayne was always *the dude*. He got a jacket real cheap from some guy on the street. It hung kind of funny on Dwayne, like it was made for somebody else, but it was still way cool. It was kind of like the jacket you have to wear if you're going to drive a Maserati some day.

"Hey, Jamel," Sammy said to me, "how do I look, man?"

"Not so cool as me," I said.

"In your face. I'm gonna be the slickest dude on the show. You watch the camera zoom in on these moves." He started doing his dance routine, bucking and strutting down the street.

"Dwayne," Sammy piped up, "if you were half as cool as you think . . ."

"Then what?" Dwayne asked, sticking out his chin.

"Then you wouldn't be walking with us, man. You'd already be driving your Maserati."

We all started laughing – except Dwayne, of course. He just kept on practicing his moves until we got right to CITY-TV. I looked around the crowd to see if Tasha was there. She said she might come down with Martina and some of the other girls, but I couldn't see any of them.

"Who you looking for?" Jo-Jo asked me.

"Nobody," I lied. "Just looking around."

The rest of them know how I feel about Tasha, and sometimes they give me a hard time about it. So I've learned to keep my mouth shut. I try to pretend I'm real cool about girls, like Dwayne is, but that's not easy when it comes to Tasha.

Up ahead, somebody opened the glass doors to the studio and the line started to move in. The

dance show starts at 3:30, but they check you in a half hour before. Dwayne pushed to the front, gave the girl his name and she ticked it off on the list. Then Jo-Jo and me got checked in, but the girl had a hard time finding Sammy on the list. Somebody goofed up his last name – like Johnson was real hard to spell or something. Finally the girl found his name under the O's and Sammy got let inside.

The studio is just a big dance floor, except it's got a couple cameras and these windows facing out on Queen Street. Leave it to Dwayne to go stick his nose in front of the cameras.

"Hey, man," Dwayne said, "maybe somebody'll see me and get me a job in the movies. You think?"

"Maybe in some kind of horror movie," Jo-Jo said in that deep voice of his.

"Yeah, you can be like Godzilla," I said.

"You kind of look like him already," Sammy added.

"You know," Dwayne said, shaking his head, "sometimes I think you guys don't appreciate me." And then he went bopping off to some music in his own head.

7

We were just waiting around for the show to start when Tasha finally came in with a bunch of her friends. She's been on the show a lot, kind of a "regular," like she says. Tasha's one of the reasons I always watch the show. Maybe she was the real reason I tried out to be here.

"Hey, Jamel, look," Sammy said to me. He gave me a nudge in the side.

"I see her, man. I see her."

"So here's your big chance, Jamel," he went on. "Show her you're really somebody."

"Yeah, sure," I said. "Fat chance." I think I felt like a somebody maybe five times in my whole life. Like the time I did that dance routine for the school show. And that one time I got a good report card, with this gold sticker on it, back in grade three. Mrs. Rhodes was my teacher then and she thought I could be special. She thought it so hard that, for a little while, I really was special.

And then all that other stuff happened. My dad got picked up and Immigration sent him back to the Islands. Me and my mom had to move to the Park, because there wasn't much money. The money's better now, but we're still there and it doesn't look like we'll ever get out.

I was thinking about all that when Dwayne stuck his head in my face. "C'mon, Jamel. You spend too much time thinking and not enough time doing. Let's go check out the girls." Dwayne was grinning at me, trying to act real cool.

So the rest of us followed him over to where Tasha stood with Sandi, Martina and a couple of girls I didn't know.

"Yo! Your dreams are answered, girls. Here we are!" Dwayne said with this big grin on his face.

The girls all groaned, except Martina who laughed, because she laughs at anything.

"Dreams or nightmares?" Tasha asked.

Sandi joined in. "Dwayne, maybe you're in the wrong place. Auditions for that new monster film are up the street."

"Real funny," Dwayne shot back. "*Real* funny. Listen, we came here to dance, not to give anybody a hard time, right?"

The girls didn't have a chance to agree. Instead, the voice of this producer guy came booming from the speakers. He told us about not blocking the cameras and not showing off and just having a good time. Then some music started and we were all supposed to dance.

I guess I should've asked Tasha right away, but I kind of waited a second too long. And then, when I was ready, she was already going off with this big dude, one of the "regular" dancers. So I danced with Martina, who's a real cool dancer anyhow.

Half an hour later, the show was going just great. The red lights on the cameras were going on and off and everybody was dancing like crazy. Even Sammy was dancing, and he's not the world's greatest.

That's when the eyes began all the trouble.

I was thinking about that later, when we got caught up in all the trouble, how it all starts with eyes. I had my eyes on Tasha, even when she was dancing with that other guy. And I could see that her eyes kept looking back at me, so that kind of told me that I had a chance with her. And then, when I really did dance with Tasha, we couldn't look

at each other, not at the same time. Our bodies, they danced together. But our eyes were real shy. And that told me something too.

But there was another kind of eye stuff going on out there. It started when Dwayne went dancing with a little white girl. I think she was Greek or Italian, or something like that, kind of short and dark. Anyway, the girl and Dwayne were laughing and having a good time. That's all.

But I saw this big white guy giving an eye to the two of them. He was one of those guys with slicked-back hair and a tight T-shirt to show off his muscles. The guy kept staring at Dwayne and the girl. He kept giving them a funny kind of look. It was the kind of look you give somebody just before you sock him in the face.

Everybody else out there dancing, they were just having a good time. Their eyes were smiling or laughing. For the couple of slow songs, their eyes were closed and dreaming. But not this guy. His eyes were real angry. It was like the little chick was his sister and he didn't want his sister dancing with a black guy.

So maybe I should have said something to Dwayne, or to the others. But who'd ever think it would get serious? They say that looks can kill, but who would ever think it could happen like that in real life?

CHAPTER 2

Your Own Kind

We all felt real good when the show was over. Dwayne kept telling us how the camera was on him all the time. Sammy kept grinning because he knew Dwayne was just shooting off his mouth. Jo-Jo was shaking his big head, since he already knew Dwayne was crazy. And I didn't say much, because I never do, but I was feeling pretty good about Tasha and me.

"The white chick gave me her number," Dwayne said, waving a scrap of paper in our faces. "Told me to call her."

"Lemme see," Sammy said, grabbing for the paper. "I bet it's the phone number for the cops. You dial that number, you get 52 Division or something."

"Or you get her old man," Jo-Jo told him. "They

don't like their girls going out with black dudes. You could get your head kicked in."

But Dwayne kept on. "You guys are just jealous," he said. "Except maybe Jamel – and that's only because he's moving in on Tasha real good."

Then they all looked at me, and there was a lot of joking around. I got embarrassed, but that just got them going even more, especially Dwayne. It was Sammy who told Dwayne to lay off, and I was glad he did. When Dwayne and Jo-Jo get going, it's enough to make me want to crawl into my running shoes.

The last thing we were thinking about was trouble. I mean, it was five o'clock on Saturday afternoon. We were going down this little street just off Queen Street. I mean, nobody would worry about getting beat up in broad daylight. But sometimes trouble just goes way out of its way to find you.

And there was trouble right up ahead. A little gang of white guys, six of 'em. I knew the first guy who shot off his mouth. It was the same greaseball who had given Dwayne the mean looks back on the dance floor. Now he had a school jacket over his T-shirt. It said Saint Something-or-other School on the jacket, and then his name: Sal.

"Hey, what's that smell?" was the first thing the guy said. It stopped our joking real fast.

"Looks like somebody let the dogs loose," came somebody else's line.

The Sal guy was staring at Dwayne just like in the studio, but he had some friends to back him up now. One of them had a baseball bat, but he didn't look like he was going to any ball game.

Dwayne didn't look scared. He stuck out his chin, the way he does sometimes. He was trying to look tough, but his lower lip was twitching. He was no match for the big dude with the angry looks. And none of us wanted to take on the guy with the baseball bat.

So I don't know why Jo-Jo had to say something. Usually, he just keeps his mouth shut and lets Dwayne do the talking. But Dwayne was looking pretty scared, and Jo-Jo didn't like that.

"You got some kind of problem, man?" Jo-Jo said.

Sal sneered at him, as if Jo-Jo weren't worth his time. "I got a problem with your friend hitting on Angela. You guys better learn to stick with your own."

"Our own what?" Jo-Jo asked.

"Your own kind," shouted one of the white guys.

That's what got Jo-Jo mad. Jo-Jo's so big he almost never gets mad, but when he does, you better watch out.

"No white garbage is gonna tell us what to do," Jo-Jo shouted. "You save that for *your* own kind."

This whole thing was making me real nervous. I started to look around for help. I mean, it wasn't like nobody could see what was going on. There were people walking up and down the street, but they all acted like they were blind. Even this little Chinese guy, out in front of his store, just went inside and shut the door.

So there was nobody on our side when the Sal guy started swearing and pushing at Dwayne. Sammy kind of blocked him, but Sal pushed past him pretty quick. Dwayne put his hands up, like he knew he was going to get hit.

The Sal guy reached out, ready to sock Dwayne, but Jo-Jo got in there first. Jo-Jo grabbed at the big guy, and for a while I thought the two of them would go at it. But then one of the other white guys pushed in, and I saw the kid with the baseball bat coming around the side.

So that's how the fight started. It wasn't real bad at first, mostly just pushing and shoving and swearing. But then somebody whomped Sammy, and Jo-Jo punched the guy in the face. That was the excuse they wanted – and then all six of them went at Jo-Jo.

I pulled one guy off my friend, and then he grabbed at me, ripping my shirt real good. I lifted my arms to push the guy's hands away and it worked, but a hunk of my shirt was still in his fingers.

That's when I went kind of crazy. I mean, it was my best shirt, the one my father sent me, and now it was just a rag. A piece of rag.

So I swung at the guy who did it. My fist connected, but not too hard. Then somebody punched me in my stomach, and I felt that one.

I doubled over and tasted blood in my mouth. There was somebody clawing at my back, trying to bring me down.

Then I felt another hand, a strong one. The hand grabbed my shoulder, flipped me around, and sent me flying sideways. I was ready to take a swing, but it wasn't a kid behind me. It was a cop.

"All right, break it up," somebody was saying.

All of a sudden, we were surrounded by four or five cops. They grabbed at us, one at a time, tossing us around. Maybe that's why cops are always so big. They can just grab you and toss you, like you're some sort of rag doll.

The cops were making their way to the middle. That's where Jo-Jo was taking on about three guys at once. Jo-Jo was bleeding from his mouth, but the white guys weren't letting up. Anybody could see it wasn't fair, even the cops.

Two of the cops pulled the white kids and tossed them away. But Sal couldn't get thrown quite so easy, so one cop pulled a nightstick and jabbed it into him. Then he used the butt of the stick to bring Jo-Jo down.

"We ought to run," Sammy said to me after we got back on our feet. He was already in plenty of trouble with the cops, and now this.

"Can't," I grunted. It was hard to talk. My lips felt all swollen up. "Jo-Jo's down and Dwayne . . . "

Then Dwayne was right beside us, the only guy who didn't get hurt. Behind us, a couple more police cars pulled up. Now there were more cops on the street than kids.

"So what's this all about?" asked some guy who wasn't even in uniform. He was talking to Jo-Jo, who was still lying kind of dazed on the sidewalk.

But it was the Sal guy who spoke up. He must've been hurting from that nightstick in the gut, but that didn't shut up his mouth.

"These black guys jumped us," he said. "They were trying to rip us off."

"Oh, man," I heard Sammy say. And I knew just what he was thinking.

CHAPTER 3

The Word Is Out

The next night we went down to the Rec Center to play some basketball, just like always.

Except it wasn't like always.

Sammy was the one who began mouthing off. "That cop didn't have to use his stick," he said, looking at Jo-Jo.

"The pigs hate us," Dwayne said. He was the only one of us who the cops didn't toss around, but that didn't stop his mouth. "They were just looking for an excuse, man."

"Yeah, but that white guy got it worse than any of us," Jo-Jo said.

"Got what he deserved," Sammy replied. "He started the whole thing, and look who the cops believed."

"The cops didn't really believe anybody," I said. "Specially with you mouthing off." I'd heard Dwayne's line too many times, how the cops are always after the black man. I guess Dwayne believed it, too. It was a line his old man used to feed him, back before his old man took off.

My old man didn't take off, he was beat by the system. It was Immigration that put him away. "Illegal immigrant" was what they called him. My mom says she told him and warned him, but my old man was kind of pig-headed. Guess he thought he could beat the system, but he got that one wrong.

So I learned something from all that – you can't beat the system, you've got to out-smart it. It's kind of like pinball. You've got play fast and smart, but don't think you can turn the whole game upside down and still win. It doesn't work like that. Of course, Dwayne was still trying to figure that one out.

"Jamel," Dwayne said to me, "you're gettin' to be a worse suck than Sammy."

"I'm just telling you how it works, man."

Sammy tried to cool the whole thing down, like always. "Listen, both of you, it ain't fair but—"

Sammy got cut off when Roger came outside the Rec Center to find us. Roger's this volunteer at the Center. He's like us, only older, maybe in his twenties. He's a big guy with bushy hair and a big space between his front teeth. Roger's got a big nose, too, which he's always sticking where it doesn't belong.

"What ain't fair?" Roger stood there holding the basketball and smiling with this dumb grin on his face.

"Nothing," I said.

"The Man," Sammy said.

"The Pigs," Dwayne said.

Jo-Jo finished it off. "My mother," he said in that deep voice of his, and then we all laughed.

Sometimes we like to talk to Roger about what happens, and sometimes we don't. Sometimes we just want to play ball. This was a night to play ball, hard.

We were up against these guys from the other end of the Park, but they weren't even close to us.

We were all charged up, all mad because of what happened. I kept feeding the ball to Jo-Jo, who'd loop it to Sammy for the lay-up. Those other guys just couldn't break the combo, not even when Roger came in to help them.

It felt good, just running and shooting, the sweat dripping down my back. Good, honest sweat that you get out of playing or working or even thinking real hard. Not like the sweat you get out of worrying. That's the kind that stinks the worst.

Jo-Jo had to go home first, because his mom still treats him like a ten-year-old. Sammy went home next because his stomach was hurting. He'd taken a punch or two in the fight and was still feeling it. Dwayne and I finished out the game with Roger on our side, then we hit the showers.

I was going to walk home with Dwayne, but Roger asked me to wait up. He said something about me helping to close up the gym, but I knew that wasn't it. I knew he was nosing around because of what he'd heard.

We finished putting the stuff away, and Roger was flipping off the lights when he started asking questions.

"So what's got to Dwayne?" Roger asked. It came out real casual, like he was asking about the weather or something. "Cop trouble?"

"Yeah," I said, looking the other way.

"Police beat him up?" he asked.

"Maybe," I said. "They laced into this white kid too, but he had it coming. He started the whole thing."

"That's what I hear," Roger said. He pulled the gym door closed and checked the lock.

"Who told you?" I asked.

"The word's out," he said. "Couple of girls this afternoon told me about the whole thing. They said you guys got charged."

"Nobody got charged," I shot back. "That's what stinks about it. It's just their word against ours. They said we tried to rob 'em. Think of that – four of us tried to rob six of them. And one of them had a baseball bat!"

I was real sarcastic, like it was some kind of

big joke, but I wasn't laughing. We'd all taken a punch or two during the fight, but nothing like the punch we got afterwards. That was a punch to our pride.

"So the cops didn't believe you?"

"Cops didn't believe anybody. We've got records. Those guys have some psycho with a baseball bat and a greaseball with a big mouth, but the cops listen to what they say. So everybody gets a warning. Man, I've had warnings all my life. Soon as your mother stops warning you, the cops start warning you."

"It doesn't stop there," Roger said. He looked at me sort of funny, like my dad used to when I was a kid. "I'll warn you too, Jamel. The word's out that those guys are coming back. They're after Dwayne, really, but they'll go after any of you."

"Not here in the Park they won't. They haven't got a chance. We've got friends."

"And you've got trouble, too," Roger replied. "Look, Jamel, I'm just saying, be careful. Watch where you're stepping, if you know what I mean."

"You mean, just because Dwayne goes dancing with this white chick, we all have to lie low?" It was crazy, I thought, just crazy.

"I'm just saying, maybe you guys have more to lose than those white kids. The cops can't get on your side unless you let them."

"The cops already had a chance to get on our side, and they blew it. Now we've got to look after ourselves. Ourselves is all we got."

"A smart guy knows when he has to look for help," Roger told me.

"Well, maybe I'm not that smart," I said right back to him. "Me and Jo-Jo and Sammy can take those guys, no sweat. We can handle it."

Roger looked like he wanted to say something else, but I didn't want to listen. I was too mad to listen to anybody right then. Whatever was coming down, I thought, we could handle it.

CHAPTER 4

All Talk, No Action

"No sweat," is what Jo-Jo said.

The four of us were sitting in the school cafeteria. Two old cafeteria ladies were eyeballing us like crazy. Tasha and her girlfriends were off in one corner. We sat at a table in the middle.

Jo-Jo just shrugged. "Those white guys think they gonna come over here and give us a rough time? Riiiight!" Of course, Jo-Jo's mother had just grounded him good, so he didn't have a thing to worry about.

"We're just gonna kick some butt if they're that stupid," Sammy bragged. The tough words sounded kind of funny coming out of him. Sammy was the smallest, the weakest of any of us. If it really came to a fight, he'd be the first to take off.

All the time the rest of us were talking, Dwayne sat there very quiet, a funny smile on his face.

"Dwayne," I asked him, "how come you got zip to say?"

"I got plenty to say," Dwayne said, looking up from his lunch. "But not about Sal and those guys. I got something to say about Angela."

"Is that the chick you were dancing with?" Jo-Jo asked.

"Yeah, that one." All of a sudden, it got about as quiet as a school cafeteria can get.

We all looked at him as if Dwayne had gone out of his mind.

"I called her number last night," Dwayne said, looking real pleased with himself.

"Yeah, so what happened?" Jo-Jo asked him. "What'd she say?"

"She didn't say a thing," Dwayne told us, "because I never got that far. I just talked to her old man – and he had lots to say."

"Like what?"

"Don't know," Dwayne said with a shrug. "It

was all in some foreign language, man. Couldn't understand a word."

That made all of us laugh, thinking about this old guy cussing out Dwayne and Dwayne not getting a word of it. Jo-Jo, he really went wild, laughing so hard I thought he'd fall right off his chair. The cafeteria ladies gave us one of those "shut up" looks, but we couldn't help it.

I guess we all needed the laugh. Things were pretty tense after I told the guys what Roger said. The word about the fight was out at school, too. Guys kept coming up, saying they'd back us up if anything happened. Not just black guys, either, but all of our friends. Nobody liked the idea of some west-end kids coming over to kick our heads in.

But it was hard to take it all seriously. I mean, all this started with Dwayne just dancing with some little Italian chick. Dwayne didn't mean anything. It wasn't like he was real hot for her, like this Angela girl was a real number for him.

But these white kids had their own ideas, or maybe they had to prove something to themselves.

I don't know. I kept on telling myself this would all blow over, that nobody could take it seriously. It was all a big stink over nothing.

After lunch, I was at my locker trying to figure out if I gave my math book to Sammy or Dwayne. When I turned around, I saw that Tasha was standing there. She had the kind of look on her face that said she wasn't sure whether she wanted to talk to me or not.

So I talked first. "Uh, hi," I said. It came out sounding kind of wimpy, so I tried again. "I mean, how's it going?"

"I heard what happened on Saturday," Tasha said.

"Yeah, I guess everybody's heard."

"It's too bad, Jamel. Because I wouldn't mind dancing with you if you're going to the show again. But I don't want to get mixed up with this gang stuff. I don't need it."

"Gang?" I said. "We aren't a gang, and we didn't start it. Even the cops figured that out."

"It doesn't matter who starts it, if it keeps going on," she said. "I don't know what Dwayne got you

guys into, but I don't want any of it. Maybe if you can find some time away from your friends, you and me can go to the show or something."

I just stared at her. For a second, I wondered if she was putting me on. Like, this was so wild that maybe Sandi or Martina made a bet to see if she could make a fool out of me. But Tasha wasn't smiling like this was a joke. She was smiling real nice, with that kind of look that makes her whole face light up. So I said, just to check, "You and me, together?"

"Yeah, but not with your friends. That Dwayne's a goof. He just likes to cause trouble. And Sammy's just dragging you down. Jo-Jo's the only one with any sense." Then she looked up at me, just for a second, kind of shy all of a sudden. "Besides you, Jamel."

I guess it took me a while to figure out that Tasha was saying she was interested in me. Maybe I'm slow upstairs, or maybe I just couldn't believe it. But there it was – I think Tasha actually asked me out.

So I should've said something cool or friendly or smart, but my mind went blank. And then the bell rang and we both had to hustle to class.

My brain wasn't on math class. My teacher, Mr. Booth, kept coming over to see if I was doing much. Then he'd look down at my workbook and see pretty much nothing. So he asked if anything was wrong, like maybe I wanted to talk to him after school.

But nothing was wrong. For once in my life, I felt like everything was going right. Tasha had just come on to me! To me!

Except I couldn't tell the guys about it, not after what she said. They'd put me down, or make fun of her, or make a joke about the whole thing. Besides, the guys were too busy looking for Sal and the west-end guys, just in case they showed up.

So I kept my mouth shut when school was over. When the four of us went outside, we had maybe twenty other guys to back us up. There were two white dudes from the football team, and a bunch of other guys from the Park. And we had a couple of crazy guys who just wanted to fight somebody, anybody.

All for nothing. I guess we were ready for cars full of kids to come racing up in front of the school, but there was nobody out there. Nobody drove up. Nothing happened. The most dangerous guys on the street were these guys in a water truck.

"All talk, man, no action," Dwayne said.

"They knew we were with you, guy," said Leroy, this football player.

"They knew we were ready to kick butt," said somebody else.

"So maybe it's over," I said. "Maybe it was no big deal after all."

"It's over for me," Dwayne said.

"How's that?" Sammy asked him.

"Angela's not worth it," he said, grinning at the rest of us. "She's too short – and I don't much like talking to her old man."

CHAPTER 5

Trouble

The thing about trouble, my mom says, is that trouble shows up when it wants to – not when you're ready for it.

When trouble came, we weren't thinking about it, we were thinking about basketball. Sammy and I were walking down Shuter, going toward the Rec Center. I guess we were joking around too, about those "tough" west-end guys and how they'd done nothing for three days now. It all seemed like a big laugh . . .

Until the car zoomed up beside us. You know the kind of car – shiny black paint, pumped-up shocks, oversized tires. It screeched to a stop, the stereo booming, and three guys jumped out.

The first two guys were just your average greaseballs. They were all bigger than me and Sammy, but didn't look too smart or too fast. I figured that we could either deke them out or outrun them if we had to.

Then Sal climbed out of the car and I started to sweat a little. He was wearing that school jacket again, with big letters saying Saint Something-or-other. I looked at him and wondered, just for a second, what Saint Something-or-other would think about all this.

Then I jabbed Sammy in the side. "Let's get out of here," I said to him.

We ran out to the street, dodged two cars that were going east, then ran down the other side-walk.

The greaseball still in the car revved up its engine. The other three guys came running after us. Just like I had guessed, they were running hard but slow. Sammy and I kept trying to put more space between them and us.

But their car was faster than our feet. It raced past us, hopped up on the sidewalk, and screeched to a stop.

Sammy zipped to one side, and I went to the

other as the driver jumped out. He came after me, running fast.

I didn't have any lead on this guy, and I was getting tired. I could feel an ache in my chest – my lungs telling me I was pushing them too hard. But the guy was right behind me, and he wasn't even breathing hard.

I've got to use my brain, I kept on telling myself. *I've got to think.* Up ahead was a house where my friend Willie Morris used to live. It's got an iron fence that Willie and I used to use for make-believe high jump. If I could still clear the thing, I figured I could leave the greaseball behind.

I had to time it just right. Off the sidewalk . . . one, two, three steps . . . hand on the top rail . . . then push, strong but easy . . .

Did it! The big dude tried to slow down to take the fence, but he couldn't do it. *Thonk!* I could hear him plowing into the fence and then him cursing.

I didn't take the time to look back. I jogged down beside the house, knocking over garbage cans to block the way. Then I zipped around in back, through Willie's old gate and out into the alley.

Which way? They were coming from the south. The Rec Center was north. They might expect me to head up that way, where maybe I could get some help. But if I turned south, I'd walk right into them. So I looked around where I was and spied a couple of sheds close together. I figured I could just barely wedge in between.

It'd be like hide-and-seek, except I'd be meat if I didn't make it home free.

I looked around and didn't see anybody. That gave me time. I pushed between the two sheds, sucking in my breath to fit. The rusty metal scraped my skin, but that was better than a busted head.

I climbed on top of a pile of old wood. I thought about that for a second, then reached down and grabbed a hunk of two-by-four. A hunk of insurance, just in case.

My breath sounded really loud. I could hear it inside my ears and bouncing off the walls of the metal sheds. It seemed so loud that anybody could hear it, so I tried to slow down my lungs. One breath, one more . . . easy and quiet. The sweat ran down my forehead and trickled from my armpits.

It felt cool while the rest of me was burning up.

I heard footsteps in the alley. They were moving fast, then they stopped. I knew it was the greaseball I'd left at the fence. He was looking for me, not sure which way to go. If I was lucky, maybe he'd just give up and go home. Maybe my tight little spot really was home free.

But then there were a bunch of voices. "Hey Marco, you seen him?"

"Lost him back here. He can't be far."

More footsteps. Lots of them. I figured all four of them were in the alley now, looking for me. If only I had a cell phone, I could have called for some help. As it was, all I had was a two-by-four in my hand. If they found me, I figured I could hurt one or two of them before they beat my head in.

One guy walked past, real quick. I could tell he didn't see me. Then two more. I stopped breathing so I wouldn't make any noise. I would've stopped my heart beating if I knew how.

Then I couldn't hear them any more. That got me real scared. It was way too quiet. They should've been making more noise. They should've –

Then I saw a face, Sal's face, staring right at mine. "We got you now," he said.

I looked the other way, but there were two guys down at that end. I was trapped between the two sheds.

"Stay back, man," I said. I was trying to sound tough, but my voice was high and shaky.

The greaseball who'd been chasing me reached in, trying to grab me. I smashed down with the two-by-four, but he pulled his arm back in time so I didn't connect.

"Tough guy, eh?" said one of them.

At the other end, I could feel them pulling at the pieces of wood beneath my feet. For a second I thought they were trying to make me fall down. But that wasn't it. No, they were getting their own weapons.

Then they pulled out an old metal pipe. It didn't take me long to figure their plan. They'd jab me with the pipe, forcing me out into the alley. Then Sal and the other greaseball would stomp me good.

I didn't have much choice but to move before

they jabbed me. I crawled sideways toward the alley, my piece of wood held high.

"Hey," Sal yelled, "he's coming out."

And I came out swinging. The one greaseball backed up, and I swung again.

That's when Sal moved in. He caught the wood after I'd swung it, twisting it from my hand. Then the first greaseball came at me. His fist connected with my side, and the pain exploded. I tried to fight back with my hands, but then Sal came at me. He slugged me once at the side of my head, and I felt myself going down –

This is it, I said to myself. *I'm never going to get up from here after they're done with me . . .*

But then some cops pulled into the alley. A cruiser roared up, then turned to block the way south. Another cop car came in at the top of the alley, then one more behind it.

Running faster than the cops was Sammy, with Roger just behind him.

Sal and the other greaseball tried to run, but there was nowhere to go. Roger came up, grabbed Sal, and had him in an arm lock faster than they can do it on TV. The cops chased down the last three greaseballs.

Sammy was mostly worried about me. "You O.K., Jamel?" Sammy asked.

"Yeah," I said, breathing again. "No problem."

"I went to get help when I saw you hop Willie's fence," Sammy told me.

"Good thing," I said. I looked around at Roger and the cops and people coming out of their backyards. Sometimes a little help is a real good thing.

CHAPTER 6

Sammy's Gun

That should have finished it. The big guy, Sal or whatever his name was, got charged. The other greaseballs got a warning from the cops. The trouble should have been all wrapped up in a Glad bag and stuck out in the garbage, if you ask me.

Except it wasn't. Somebody told Dwayne that the west-end kids had friends, and now the friends were after us. Somebody else said a bunch of Saint Something-or-other kids jumped a black guy downtown. Jo-Jo thought he saw the greaseball's black car cruising near our school. Word was that Sal had some smart lawyer who was going to beat the charge for him.

So I was still pretty tense. A lot of guys at school were talking about fights between blacks and whites. Of course, there were all kinds of other fights, black against black, white against white. But nobody talked about those. It was the racial fights that got even the teachers going, like when Ahmed got his head kicked in by Franco. And when a kid called Bug-eyes got bloodied by that geek John Lewin. Teachers had a lot to say about "racial understanding." They even got somebody in from City Hall to give us all a talk.

I tried to keep my nose out of all this. I didn't need any more trouble. I talked to Tasha a couple times, and that was nice. It was a lot better than worrying about fights and white kids giving me rude looks. When I saw Tasha, it was like everything else was all stupid and ugly, but the two of us were something special.

It took a while, but finally she said we could go to the dance show together at the end of June—if everything stayed cool. That was her deal, and it seemed plenty good to me.

So I didn't appreciate it when Sammy turned up the temperature.

We were at his place, one of those low-rise buildings at the south end of the Park. His mom was off working at the hospital, so we had the place to ourselves. Sammy had this rap music going real loud, because his mom wasn't home. Up on the walls I could see all these pictures of his dad.

Sammy's old man was a musician, played the trumpet way back when. His dad used to think he could make it big time, kind of like Wynton Marsalis. The old guy even had a couple tapes out on some small label. But Sammy's father had a heart attack before he could make it big time. He checked out before anybody knew if he was all that good. Now Sammy was in the Park with the rest of us, and he couldn't play a note of music if he had to. It didn't seem fair, but that's how it was.

"Got to show you something, Jamel," Sammy said to me.

"What?"

"Protection," he said, with this funny look on his face.

Sammy went back to his bedroom, then came out with this beat-up old box. I figured maybe he bought himself a knife or something. I used to carry this little pocket knife to school, back a couple of years ago. But then I figured out that I'd never get the thing out fast enough to use it in a fight.

But Sammy had more than just a knife hidden in the box. He pulled off some rags and showed me.

"Holy –," I said. "Where'd you get a gun, Sammy?"

"From this guy I know. On the street."

I lifted the gun up. It was heavy and cold, still a little oily. I didn't really know how to hold the thing, but it felt good in my hands. There was a kind of power in it that you could feel in the weight and the oily metal.

"You know how to use this thing?" I asked. I kept thinking I might pull the trigger, just by accident, and put a hole right through my best friend's head.

Sammy just shrugged. "I know enough."

"So what you gonna do with this? Carry it with you all the time?"

"Maybe," Sammy replied. "But mostly when I

need it, you know? Like what if Sal and those guys tried to break in here?"

"Nobody's that stupid," I said. "Besides, you just have to call the cops – "

"So think about this. What if we didn't find you in that alley, Jamel? Sal and those guys could've killed you. But not if you got a gun. Nobody messes with you if you got a gun."

"I don't know, Sammy," I said, shaking my head. "You can't go running down the street with the thing hanging off your belt. Or if somebody gives you a look, you can't just put a hole through his head. I mean, if you shoot somebody, you're the one in trouble. And the cops will just use this like an excuse, man. They even sniff a gun, and you're meat."

"I'm not worried about the cops," Sammy said. "I'm worried about that guy Sal." He reached out and took the gun out of my hand. "Since Jo-Jo's been grounded, we don't have much muscle on our side. We just got you, me and Dwayne."

"You're crazy," I said. "There's plenty of guys on our side. We don't need a gun."

Sammy just stared at me. I could tell by looking at him that he wasn't crazy. He was scared, like me, like all of us, deep down. When they're scared, some guys start acting tough, like Dwayne. Some guys try to put their mind on something else, like me. Some guys have got enough guts to say that they're scared, like Jo-Jo. And some guys – more and more of them – just go get a gun.

"Sammy, I don't like this," I said, handing the gun back to him.

"Me neither," Sammy said. "But we have to look after our own, you know? We can't just let them push us around."

CHAPTER 7

Going to the Rally

Then it all hit the fan. Dwayne came running up to me when I got to school next day.

"Yo, Jamel, you hear about it?"

"Hear about what?"

"About the cops. They shot another black guy last night."

"In Los Angeles?"

"No, man, right here, right off Bay Street. The dude didn't have a gun or anything, but they still shot him."

I just shook my head. The cops in Toronto had already shot four black guys this year. That's what the paper said, and this guy would be number five. "Drug dealers," that's what they call the guys. "Tried to escape arrest," that's what they say. But five black men had been shot down since the year began, and people were starting to ask questions.

"It's getting bad, man," I said.

"There's a big rally down at City Hall tonight." Dwayne's voice was up real high, like it gets when he's all excited. "We've got to show some muscle, Jamel. If we don't, every black guy in this town is going to end up a walking target for the cops."

"You talk to Sammy and Jo-Jo?"

"Yeah, Sammy's coming but Jo-Jo's still grounded. His mom is one tough old lady."

"So the rest of us can go to it, man," I told him. "We've got to get ourselves some respect!"

The words sounded kind of funny after I said them. I mean, if the cops hadn't come zooming into that alley, I wouldn't be in any shape to come to school. And if the cops hadn't stopped that fight after the dance show, it would have cost me more than a ripped shirt.

Back when I was a kid, I even wanted to be a cop someday. I used to think about looking real cool in the uniform and swinging my nightstick at bad guys. That's the kind of thing that goes through a kid's head.

But I'm sixteen now, and I know it isn't so simple. I've seen how cops really work. I've read how a white guy at a dot.com can rip off a million bucks, and he gets a rap on the knuckles. But let some black guy try to rip off a milk store for a couple bucks and, boom, he's blown away. That's how it works – and maybe the rally would help make it stop.

The guys were talking about the rally all day. Not just black guys, but white dudes too. Maybe the hot weather was making everybody a little crazy, but that's how it was. There was this kind of tension in the air. Dwayne called it "electricity," like they say in the old movies, but it was more than that. It's like we all knew something was going to happen, something big, and we wanted to be there.

So maybe that's how I got the guts to go up to Tasha at afternoon break. I mean, I knew how she felt about gangs and trouble and all that, but this was different. This was about being black and standing up for yourself. This was about respect.

"So you going to the rally tonight?" I asked her, kind of cool.

"I don't know," she said, looking right at me. "Martina wants to go, but my mom won't like it."

"She lets you go downtown to dance, but not for something that matters?" I guess I had that kind of look on my face.

"Yeah, I know it's stupid, but – "

"So how about you go with me? I mean, if your mom will let you. That way, if there's any trouble, you know, I can – "

Tasha cut me off. "If there's trouble, Jamel, I'll be the one to protect *you*. It won't be the other way around."

"That's O.K. too," I said, smiling at her. "The way things been going lately, I might need a little help. So I'll come by at six maybe?"

"Six-thirty," she replied. "And don't bring your friends. I'll have enough to do looking after you, Jamel."

All that sounded plenty good to me. I knew that Sammy and Dwayne would give me a hard time about it, but that's life. Besides, Tasha and I could meet them down at the rally, kind of by accident. At least, that's what I said to Sammy.

Sammy and I were walking home together after school. We always walked in two's now, just in case

60

Sal and his friends showed up. I told Sammy about going to the rally with Tasha and he just gave me this smile.

"You're going to do just fine with her, Jamel," he said. "You're turning into quite the hustler."

That got me a little embarrassed so I looked down at my feet. It didn't seem to me that a real hustler would be wearing beat-up size thirteen Nikes. Then again, I wasn't a real hustler.

"So listen, man," he said. "Where do we just run into you two – by accident, of course."

"How about in front of Old City Hall? You know, the place they use for the courthouse." Our class had done a field trip down there last month. I guess the teachers wanted to scare us into staying out of jail. All I figured out is that going to court is pretty slow and pretty boring.

"O.K.," Sammy said, "we'll be on the steps. Just by accident." He gave met this look, like it was all planned out.

"Right," I said, turning off to my building.

"And Jamel," he called out, "don't worry about nothin'. I'm bringing my protection."

I turned back to say something, but Sammy was already bopping off to his building. I let him go. I didn't know exactly what to say anyhow. Except that I didn't want protection that you have to keep oiled and loaded.

CHAPTER 8

No Justice, No Peace

Tasha knew right away that it was no "accident" when we met Dwayne and Sammy. But that didn't matter much because she brought Martina along. So it wasn't like we were going out or anything. It was just the five of us, all together, all down at the rally.

When we got there, there were a bunch of guys up on a stand in front of City Hall. I guess they were mostly politicians, a lot of them black. They were yelling and screaming into a mike, but the sound system didn't work quite right. All the yelling came out scratchy, like a CD player if you stuck a pen through the speakers. Sammy did that to mine once, so I know.

But we didn't care much, because the crowd was really what it was about. Some guy up in front would scream something, and we'd all shout, "Right on!" Or we'd do this chant – "No justice, no peace" – over and over again. I guess the crowd was maybe half white, half black, but it didn't matter. These white dudes kept on calling us "brother" and shouting "No more white justice," just as loud as we were.

All the time, I had a smell, or taste, or worry that said that something was going to happen. We all knew it. I think even Tasha felt it. We were pressed pretty tight in the crowd, and I could feel that she was nervous.

Dwayne and Sammy were up in front, shouting with all the rest of them. Sammy had a sports bag looped over his arm. It seemed like a funny thing to bring to a rally, but I knew why Sammy had it. I knew what was in it.

One time this police guy came to the mike. He tried to say something about how cops need guns. He tried to tell us how the shooting wasn't a race thing, because a black cop had shot a black guy. But nobody listened to him. We booed and hissed and cussed until he gave up and sat down. We wasn't gonna listen to that kind of stuff. We wanted to get pumped up.

The next guy at the mike really got it going. He was an old black dude with Rasta dreadlocks, but could he ever lay into the cops. "We're sick of white justice," he shouted. "We're sick of white judges and white juries and white cops. We're sick of what they do to black people. We just want to tell the whole world – it's not open season on black people anymore!"

Then the crowd went wild, yelling and screaming. The chant started up again – "No justice, no peace" – and we all started moving. We were going east, toward the Eaton Centre. Somebody else said we'd go up Yonge Street. But nobody really knew what it was all about. We just moved, all together, like we all had one brain.

Except Tasha, who pulled on my T-shirt. "Jamel," she shouted over all the noise, "I don't like this."

"Don't like what?" I shouted back.

"How this is going," she told me. "I was O.K. with the rally, but this has turned into something else. This is going to get mean."

"It's just a march, Tasha," I told her with a shrug. "It's a protest, that's all."

"I still don't like it."

"So what are you going to do?" I asked her. "Are you going to call 911 on your cell? I'll tell you, the cops are already here. Or maybe you're going to try to walk the other way, eh?"

Around us, thousands of people were all pressed together, moving one way. No way somebody could go against that.

"Jamel – " she called out.

"Besides," I cut her off, "you're the one who is supposed to protect me, remember?"

Tasha didn't say any more. I knew she wasn't happy about this, but she didn't try to leave either. The five of us were all caught in the center of the crowd. And the crowd was moving fast toward Eaton Centre.

Except the guys at Eaton Centre were too smart for us. They locked up their doors early, just like the Bay across the street. So when we got there, there was nothing to do but turn up Yonge.

Dwayne and Sammy and Martina were up in

front. They kept chanting, "Our cops ain't tops," and had their fists up in the air. It was kind of like a rock concert, but a concert that moved right up the street.

I got into it too. "No more white justice! No justice, no peace!"

Tasha hit me with her elbow to stop me from shouting out. "Jamel," she said, "I'm getting out of this."

I just looked at her. Weren't we all in it together – brothers and sisters, blacks and whites?

But she had her mind made up. "I'm going to duck down into the subway at College Street. Are you coming with me or are you going to wait around till trouble starts?"

I didn't know what to say. Part of me wanted to go with her, and maybe the two of us could stay together and have a good time. But part of me wanted to stay, wanted to be part of the action. I guess my mouth was still hanging open, kind of stupid-looking, when the first glass broke.

We all heard it. Somebody smashed a store

window, maybe with a brick or a rock. All of a sudden, there was a big hole in the glass of some cheap stereo store.

A dozen guys began pushing from behind us. They all wanted to get to the window, to see what was happening, or maybe grab something for themselves. Then a bunch of guys started reaching into the window, grabbing tapes and phones and other stuff. Other guys started shouting, "What you doing, man?" but that didn't stop them. Even Dwayne got into it.

"Hey, man, I want some too," he said, pushing toward the front.

But he didn't get very far. There were plenty of guys at that store window, grabbing and fighting each other for the stuff. And the biggest guy up there was a guy we all knew.

It was Sal, the guy with St. Something-or-other on his jacket.

CHAPTER 9

Sal Is Back

I don't know how Sal saw me. There had to be a thousand guys there, a thousand faces staring at him. But somehow he looked right at me. His eyes just picked out my face, and we looked at each other for about a second.

"That's that Sal guy!" Sammy shouted to me.

"Yeah. He's probably got his whole gang with him." I looked around to see if I could pick out any of the others.

"What are you guys talking about?" Tasha asked.

"Nothing" I lied. "Just some guy we know." But Sammy and I were both trying to push back into the crowd, away from Sal. I guess we both thought there was trouble enough without those guys, too.

But Dwayne wasn't paying any attention. I guess he was busy thinking about going up and grabbing some stuff for himself. Dwayne's like that sometimes, kind of pushy. He'll see other kids with stuff he wants, some kind of Walkman or cool jacket or something, and it makes him act kind of crazy.

But I guess everybody was a little crazy that day.

Up ahead, I saw some guys go up to a hot dog cart and flip the thing upside down. They didn't have any reason. It wasn't that the hot dog guy had any money, or they wanted to rip off some food. It was just that he was there, and they felt like doing something. It seemed like everybody in the crowd was getting crazier and crazier.

Way up ahead, I could see a bunch of cops walking in front of the crowd. It looked like they were clearing the way for us. They were getting people off the sidewalks, telling stores to close up. But there were no police around us. There was nobody to stop what these guys were doing.

When the crowd got up to College Street, Tasha grabbed my arm. She wanted to get out of this.

"I'm leaving, Jamel. The subway's just up ahead. Are you coming with me or what?"

This time I didn't argue. The whole rally and march were getting sort of ugly. I couldn't see that Sal guy any more, but I knew he was around. And Dwayne was pushing way up ahead, waiting for the next window to get smashed in. I didn't want any of that stuff. Dwayne could get himself busted for B&E if that's what he wanted, but I had had enough.

Tasha and Martina and I pushed our way out to the edge of the crowd. I kept looking around for Sal, but didn't see him again. I didn't see anybody I knew, just a bunch of faces, all of them with this crazy look.

We were almost out of the crowd when this old drunk white guy started yelling at us.

"Go back home. Go back where you come from you black —" I won't give you all the swear words that came after.

Of course, we weren't all black. We were black and brown and white and every color in between, but nobody was going to explain that to the old drunk. He'd mouthed off at the wrong spot at the wrong time.

"What you say?" somebody yelled back.

"I said, you're all a bunch of – " and then he started cussing us. He waved his fist at the crowd, like he was going try something.

A kid in a red bandanna walked up to the guy.

"What you call me?"

The guy was way too drunk to back off. "I says you're – "

The kid didn't let him finish. He hit the drunk guy hard, right in the gut. The old guy fell down and then there were four others on top of him. A couple guys were hitting his head. A couple more were grabbing at his jacket and pulling his pockets out to see if he had money.

Some of the whites on the sidewalk were shouting, "Leave him alone," but nobody did much right away.

The old guy could've been real beat up, but a bunch of black guys from my school pushed up front. I knew a couple of them – Leroy Williams and Josh Marshall from the football team. It was Leroy who took the first kid, pasted him in the face, and said, "Leave the drunk be." It was Josh who picked up the drunk, dusted him off, and sent him staggering down the sidewalk.

When it was over, Tasha and Martina really got on my case. "We've got to get out of here," Martina said, and she sounded plenty scared.

So we had almost ducked into the subway when the cops showed up.

All of a sudden there was a whole army of cops. Some were on horses, coming over from Bay Street. Others came pouring up from the subway and from the side streets. They were all dressed in riot gear – helmets and shields and nightsticks ready.

"Break up and go home," came this voice. "The rally is over. You are ordered to break up and go home."

But we couldn't get home. There was this line of cops coming at us, blocking the way to the subway. The crowd couldn't go anywhere, but the cops kept coming in a wedge. They had their nightsticks ready to club anybody who didn't move.

So we pushed back, away from the subway. Tasha grabbed me and I grabbed Martina and we pushed north up Yonge. The whole crowd began running now. We had been crazy angry before. Now we were crazy scared. People kept pushing each other. Some guys would fall down, but nobody stopped to help them up. People would step over them, or right on top of them, trying to get away.

The cops were coming at us from one side. Store windows kept breaking on the other. The three of us were stuck in the middle.

At Charles Street, we made a break to the east. The crowd was splitting up into little groups now, running between stores or down alleys. Some of the guys still had boom boxes, or DVDs, or jackets they'd ripped off from the stores. The cops were right about one thing – we weren't a rally any more. We were just a bunch of scared kids, trying to get someplace that wasn't crazy.

It was in an alley behind Yonge where we saw

Sal one more time. I spotted the St. Something-or-other jacket first, then saw his face. He was bent over, punching some kid. It took me a second or two to figure out that I knew the kid who was taking the punches.

It was Dwayne!

CHAPTER 10

Put the Gun Down

Sal was punching Dwayne, grabbing at a leather jacket that Dwayne must have ripped off from a store. There were three or four white kids watching this, but nobody was trying to stop it.

So I let go of Martina and raced over. I figured if I got up enough speed I could knock Sal right off his feet, and then . . . then I didn't know what. But I couldn't let him keep beating on Dwayne. I couldn't.

I ran like crazy, then came tearing into Sal, hitting him with my shoulder. I sent him flying, right off Dwayne and onto the ground.

I looked down and saw that Dwayne's face was all messed up. There was blood running down his nose and onto this T-shirt. Some of the blood was running down onto his new jacket.

Then a funny thing happened. I was in the middle of all this, breathing hard, wondering if somebody was gonna jump on my back. And for a second it all stopped, like a freeze-frame in a movie. All I did was look down at the ripped-off leather jacket and think, *That blood is going to ruin it,* I thought. *The jacket won't be worth two cents.*

It was Tasha's voice that snapped me out of it.

"Jamel, watch out!" I heard.

I looked over my shoulder. There was Sal, up on his feet. He was coming at me like a bulldozer in high gear.

I looked around real quick, trying to figure out what to do. Sal was bigger than me and weighed a lot more than I did. I couldn't take him one-on-one. And I sure wouldn't last long if he laced into me.

But maybe I could buy some time.

I jerked to the left just before Sal got to me. Then I kicked out, catching him in the right leg. Sal went down again and swore at me.

"C'mon, Dwayne," I said, grabbing my friend's arm. "We've got to get out of here."

"Yeah man, sure," Dwayne said. But there was this glassy look in his eyes, like he wasn't really there.

I pulled at his arm, but Dwayne wasn't working with me. He kept flopping back down to the ground, so I couldn't keep hold.

"C'mon, man. You've got to get up," I said.

Then Tasha came over and kneeled down the other side of Dwayne. She pulled at one arm while I pulled at the other until we got him sitting up.

"Jamel —" I heard. This time it was Martina's voice, but I didn't get the message quick enough.

Bam! Sal was on me. He walloped me right in the head. I saw these little white specks for a second, and then there was a burst of heat.

I was nowhere. It was like my head was floating up in the air, burning, but floating up with the white specks. And then he hit me again, and I was down on the ground.

The next thing I heard was a lot of screaming. I don't know how long I was out – maybe not long at all. But when I could hear something, it was screaming and shouting. The noise didn't come from me or Dwayne or Tasha, it came from the guys around us.

Over it all, I heard a voice I knew. It was Sammy's voice, scared but tough.

"Get away from them. Get back."

I couldn't figure it out. Everybody was pulling back. Even Sal wasn't on top of me any more. He was over beside us, on his knees, looking like he'd seen St. Something-or-other himself standing right in front of us.

I couldn't figure it out until I saw Sammy standing there. He was holding the gun in his hand.

"What are you doing?" I yelled at him. Then my head hurt and I felt kind of dizzy.

The gun was shaking in Sammy's hand, like sometimes it was pointed at me and sometimes at Sal.

"Listen, man," Sal said, his voice real low. "Just take it easy. I didn't mean nothing." He was moving on his knees, real slow, trying to get behind the three of us.

"Leave them alone," Sammy shouted. "Don't get near 'em. Don't you move – "

Then everything went crazy. Sal tried to jump behind us, and Sammy gritted his teeth, and Tasha shouted something.

And the gun exploded.

It was loud, so loud I couldn't hear for a long time. It seemed like the only thing in my head was the echo of the gun shot.

Then the screaming started. I kept looking around, trying to figure out who got shot. Sal looked O.K., and I didn't feel anything, and Tasha was just kind of crying. But Sammy had this awful look on his face. His mouth was open, like he wanted to say something, but no words came out.

Then I looked down and saw. I saw why Tasha was crying and everybody else was screaming. There was this red splotch on Dwayne chest.

"You shot Dwayne!" I screamed. "You stupid jerk – you shot Dwayne!"

Sammy just seemed frozen. He was holding the gun like he might shoot it again, but he was frozen.

"Put the gun down," I shouted at him. "Put it down."

And maybe that saved a couple guys right then,

I don't know. They told me later that some cop already had his gun out, aimed at Sammy. They say that Sammy might have killed himself unless he put the gun down. Or maybe Sammy would have tried to shoot at Sal again, and who knows which one of us he would have hit.

But none of that happened. Sammy lowered the gun and I turned back to Dwayne. There was all this blood pouring out of him. It came pumping out like crazy. I took the leather jacket and pressed it against the hole in his chest. I kept trying to stop the blood, trying to keep the blood inside him.

"Dwayne," Tasha said, her voice real low. "Hang in there for us."

Dwayne was still staring up, but it was like he wasn't seeing us.

"Dwayne, say something, man," I cried. "Let me know you're still there."

But Dwayne said nothing, nothing at all.

CHAPTER 11

Stupid Things Add Up

So maybe you read about it in the paper. The big riot on Yonge Street. How this black guy got shot in the chest. How this other black guy got all kind of charges laid on him. How the "protest turned into a rampage" or "the crowd acted like animals."

Those were the headlines. Those were the six o'clock news stories.

But the real story isn't like that. The real story is about my friend Sammy, who was just a scared kid, like most of us. The real story is about a kid who buys a gun because he's scared, and then he's stupid enough to use it. The real story is about the way friends can hurt each other, by accident. It was an accident, wasn't it?

We went to Dwayne's funeral, Tasha and me together. Jo-Jo came with his mom and Roger from the Rec Center. Almost all the kids from school were there, too.

The funeral was real awful. Dwayne's mom was crying and the minister kept carrying on about the "tragedy." There were all kinds of politicians there too. They were making speeches about "racial understanding," mostly for the TV news crews.

Let me tell you – I don't know so much about "racial understanding." All I know is that I've got one friend who's dead and one friend who's in jail. And there's this guy Sal who started the whole thing, but not much has happened to him.

It doesn't seem fair to me. Maybe life isn't fair. Or maybe all the little stupid things that we did – from the fight to the gun to the rally – maybe they all added up. Maybe that's the math – all these little stupid things add up to one guy dead on the street. I don't know.

Roger tells me that I've got to get over it. He says I've got to make plans for my own life and do something good with it. Tasha tells me the same thing.

All I can say is that I'm trying. I know the fighting and the hate and the fear, they got us nowhere. So somehow we've all got to get smarter. Somehow we've all got to do better.

Here are some other titles you might enjoy:

Tag Team by PAUL KROPP

Jes had plenty of problems to start with. He was short, shy and lonely – at least until he went out for the school's wrestling team. Then his life seemed to turn around – until he had to deal with Banjo and Joey down in the tunnel.

My Broken Family by **PAUL KROPP**

Divorce is always rotten. When Maddy's parents split up, her whole life starts to fall apart. Maddy holds on to her dancing as one thing that is really hers. But when it's all over, she finds that love is stronger than she thought.

Scarface by PAUL KROPP

Coming to Canada had been a great thing for Tranh. This was a country of peace and wealth and happiness. So why did Martin Beamis keep picking on him? Did this rich kid have nothing better to do than make life rotten for someone who had already suffered so much?

Hitting the Road by **PAUL KROPP**

The road isn't nice to kids who run away. Matt knew there would be trouble even before he took off with his friend Cody. Along the way, there would be fighting, fear, hunger and a jump from a speeding train. Was it all worth it?

About the Author

Paul Kropp is the author of many popular novels for young people. His work includes six award-winning young-adult novels, many high-interest novels, as well as writing for adults and younger children.

Mr. Kropp's best-known novels for young adults, *Moonkid and Prometheus* and *Moonkid and Liberty,* have been translated into German, Danish, French, Portuguese and two dialects of Spanish. They have won awards both in Canada and abroad. His most recent books are *The Countess and Me* and four picture books for young readers based on CBC's Mr. Dressup series.

Paul Kropp lives with his wife, Lori Jamison, in an 1889 townhouse in Toronto's Cabbagetown district. He has three sons (Alex, Justin and Jason) and three step-children (Emma, Ken and Jennifer).

**For more information, see the author's website at
www.paulkropp.com**

For more information on the books in the New Series Canada, contact:

High Interest Publishing – Publishers of H•I•P Books
407 Wellesley Street East • Toronto, Ontario M4X 1H5
www.hip-books.com